TITAN A.E.

STORYBOOK

Adapted by Jennifer Frantz

HarperCollins*Entertainment*
HarperCollins*Entertainment* is an imprint of HarperCollins*Publishers*

TITAN A.E. TM & © 2000 Twentieth Century Fox Film Corporation. All rights reserved. Published in the USA
by Price Stern Sloan, a member of Penguin Putnam Books for Young Readers, New York. Printed in the USA.
First published in Great Britain by HarperCollins*Entertainment* in 2000. HarperCollins*Entertainment* is an
imprint of HarperCollinsPublishers Ltd, 77-85 Fulham Palace Road, Hammersmith, London W6 8JB
The HarperCollins website address is www.**fire**and**water**.com

ISBN 0 00 710314 X

Conditions of Sale

EARTH, 3028

"Dad, my invention broke," grumbled a frustrated Cale Tucker. His latest invention had just spun off wildly down the river.

Sam Tucker picked up his son and brushed his cheek gently. "Later, Cale. We have to go now."

Just over the hill, humans and aliens were rushing toward thousands of rocket ships.

"Professor Tucker," someone shouted, "the Drej have breached the global defense system!" It was Tek, an alien friend of Sam's.

Sam hoisted Cale quickly into the hover jeep and jumped in. They sped off toward one of the ships.

"I have to go on a different ship," Sam told his son. "Tek is going to look after you."

"But I wanna go with you!" Cale cried.

"It's not safe where I am going," Sam said as he slipped his ring on Cale's finger. "I want you to always keep this. I will see you again." Sam kissed his son, and then he was gone.

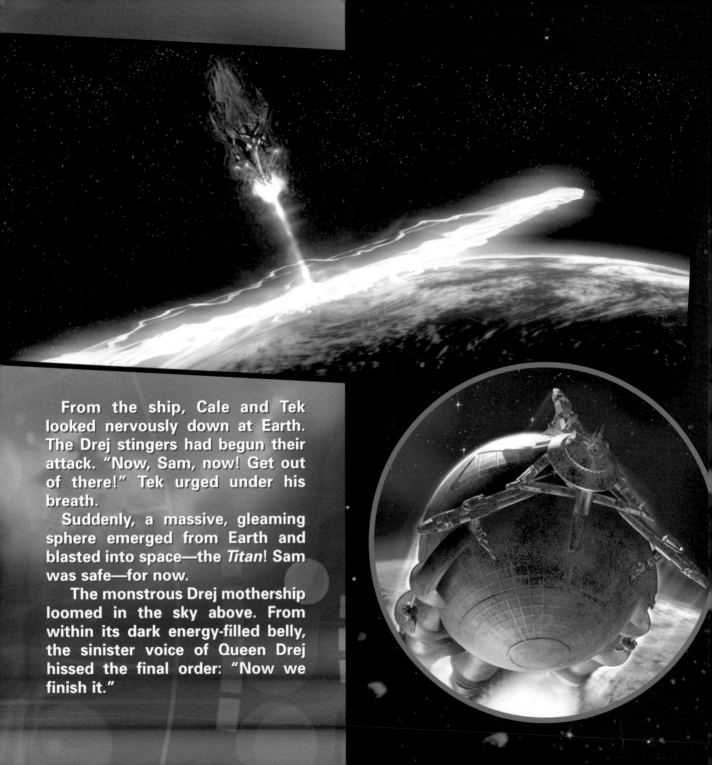

From the ship, Cale and Tek looked nervously down at Earth. The Drej stingers had begun their attack. "Now, Sam, now! Get out of there!" Tek urged under his breath.

Suddenly, a massive, gleaming sphere emerged from Earth and blasted into space—the *Titan*! Sam was safe—for now.

The monstrous Drej mothership loomed in the sky above. From within its dark energy-filled belly, the sinister voice of Queen Drej hissed the final order: "Now we finish it."

In a beam of cold blue light, Earth was riddled with jagged cracks. Then came an enormous explosion of fiery gas, hurtling rock, and blinding light.

And then, Earth was gone.

TAU-14
15 YEARS LATER

"**T**hat's lunch! One hour," barked the alien foreman.

Cale, now grown up, busted through the pack to the front of the line.

"*Humans* wait," the foreman snapped, pushing Cale into a group of humans in the back.

"Don't count on it. I'm taking the express," Cale announced as he took off towards the docks on his scooter. "The odds of a ship docking are a thousand to one!"

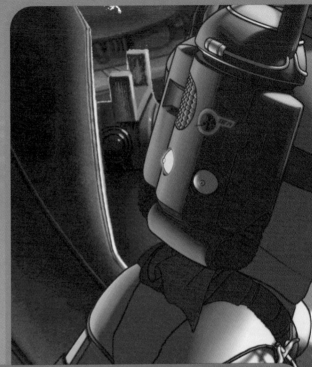

"And that would be the one!"

A huge ship crunched Cale's scooter and sent him reeling into the air.

When his gravity boots landed him on the ship's giant windscreen, Cale peered in to see who had hit him. His eyes locked on a beautiful girl seated in the pilot's chair.

Embarrassed, Cale tried to play off his blunder. He casually pulled out a handkerchief and began wiping the glass. The girl glanced at him, then coolly pressed a button that blocked out the windscreen *and* Cale.

Later in the commissary, Cale was sitting with Tek when a man sat down at their table. Cale immediately didn't like his attitude. "Tek, who *is* this guy?" Cale asked suspiciously.

"Joseph Korso," the man replied. "I was with your father on the *Titan* project. You still have that ring your father gave you?" he asked, snatching it swiftly from Cale's hand. He tapped the ring with a pen and it began to glow. "Put it on Cale."

Suddenly, an unusual pattern covered Cale's palm.

"It's a map," said Korso. "Your father hid the *Titan* where the Drej couldn't find it. Well, no one can. Except you."

"It's time to stop running," Tek added, looking at Cale.

"Well, actually," said Korso, eyeing the door, "I think it's time to start."

"Drej!" Cale cried. "What do they want?"

"They want you, kid. Same way I want you, only dead," Korso replied.

Korso and Cale took off. Dodging Drej fire, they reached a fightercraft and jumped in.

The Drej were right on their tails blasting furiously, and the bay doors were about to lock down. Korso sped the fightercraft toward the rapidly closing doors. They weren't going to make it! At the last second, Korso hit the eject button, shooting the escape pod away from the fightercraft. It smashed through the glass ceiling of the docking arm out into space. They were safe... until they noticed a crack spreading in the glass windscreen of the pod! They didn't have much time.

"Akima we need a pick up!" Korso shouted into his radio.

THE VALKYRIE

Cale awoke and found himself on a table. Akima, the girl from the dock, was examining him, and so was a strange alien she called Preed.

"Cross half of the galaxy," Akima grumbled, "just so we can rescue the window washer."

"Hey," Cale protested, "for your information, I happen to be humanity's last great hope."

Preed looked very unimpressed.

"I mean, I'm the guy with the map here," Cale continued and held up his hand.

Akima gently touched his hand. "This is really it. This can save us . . . "

"Korso wants Gune to check the map," interrupted Preed.

They took Cale to see Gune, the brilliant, muttering alien navigator. Preed showed him Cale's hand. Gune's large eyes began examining the map closely. "Ahh . . . the broken moon of Sesharrim. Only thirteen thousand keks away."

"Have Akima lay in a course," commanded Korso.

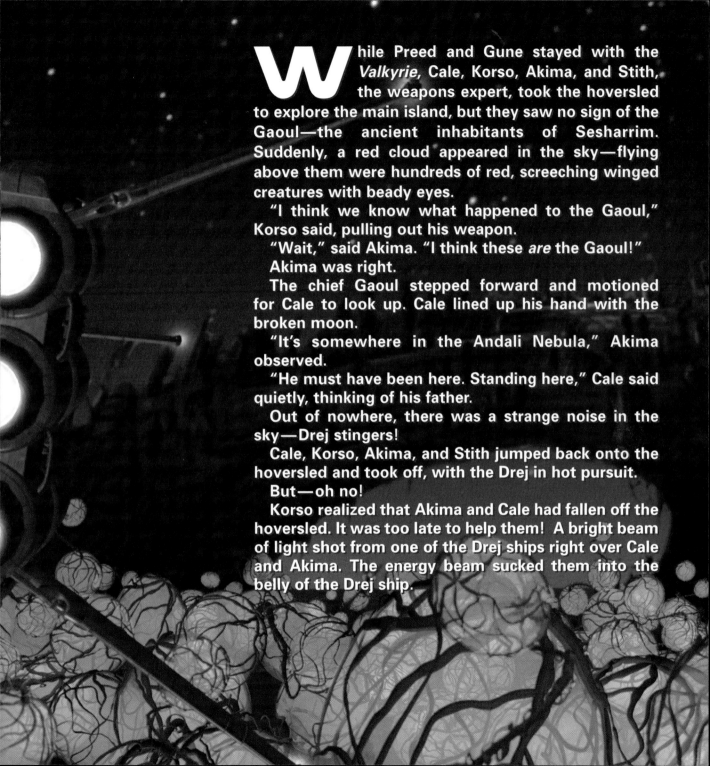

While Preed and Gune stayed with the *Valkyrie*, Cale, Korso, Akima, and Stith, the weapons expert, took the hoversled to explore the main island, but they saw no sign of the Gaoul—the ancient inhabitants of Sesharrim. Suddenly, a red cloud appeared in the sky—flying above them were hundreds of red, screeching winged creatures with beady eyes.

"I think we know what happened to the Gaoul," Korso said, pulling out his weapon.

"Wait," said Akima. "I think these *are* the Gaoul!"

Akima was right.

The chief Gaoul stepped forward and motioned for Cale to look up. Cale lined up his hand with the broken moon.

"It's somewhere in the Andali Nebula," Akima observed.

"He must have been here. Standing here," Cale said quietly, thinking of his father.

Out of nowhere, there was a strange noise in the sky—Drej stingers!

Cale, Korso, Akima, and Stith jumped back onto the hoversled and took off, with the Drej in hot pursuit.

But—oh no!

Korso realized that Akima and Cale had fallen off the hoversled. It was too late to help them! A bright beam of light shot from one of the Drej ships right over Cale and Akima. The energy beam sucked them into the belly of the Drej ship.

akima struggled as the Drej pinned her against the wall with an energy force. Cale lunged to help her, but he was shot into the air by a beam of light. It held him there as the map in his hand began to glow. The Drej were reading the map!

Finally, Queen Drej said with a sinister hiss, "We have our destination. Set a course for the Nebula. Keep the boy on board. Discard the girl."

"Akima!" Cale cried, but it was too late.

Akima was encased in a strange glass pod, which was sucked through the wall of the ship and sent out into open space.

Cale was pulled through the floor into a cell that pulsed with electric energy.

TRADER COLONY:
SOROS

The remaining crew of the *Valkyrie* tracked Akima to Soros, where human slave traders had taken her.

"Come along, you worthless speck of human pocket lint!" barked Preed, who was pretending to be a slave trader, at Korso, who was pretending to be a slave.

The alien guard, however, didn't buy their act. "He's not a slave, and you're not traders."

Thinking quickly, Stith swiftly knocked the guard aside with a strong kick. The crew rushed in, found Akima's cell, and blasted the lock off, freeing her.

DREJ SHIP

Cale touched the strange blue wall and was blasted backwards from the shock. That hurt! There was a flash of color where his hand touched it. Braving the horrible shock, Cale put both hands into the energy field and brought them together. His hands were penetrating the energy, creating a window. Cale painfully forced his body through the energy field.

Escaping down a hallway, Cale overheard the Drej queen as she said, "Prepare forces to destroy the *Titan*!" Cale took off with a new determination.

While in the hangar of the ship, Cale saw a Drej stinger landing nearby. He rolled under the ship. It was dangerous, but Cale thought he could successfully control the energy of the stinger, as he had with the cell wall.

Gradually, the ship began to rise from the floor—with Cale at the controls! He peeled out of the hangar with a swarm of other stingers. He wanted desperately to locate the *Valkyrie.*

As Cale approached his destination in the Drej stinger, he tried to signal to the crew. Just as Stith took aim, Gune caught the signal and cried—"It's Cale!"

With Cale safely back in the navigation room, Gune examined the map again. "The map is different," he announced. "Yes, it's very, very clear. These are the Ice Rings of Tigrin," Gune explained pointing at a pulsing spot on Cale's hand.

"Then I guess we're back in business," said Korso, giving Cale an intense look.

THE VALKYRIE
DRIFTER COLONY: NEW BANGKOK

after waking from a bad dream, Cale went to Akima's room for some company.

He looked around at all of the knickknacks from Earth that decorated her room. "Where'd you get all this junk?" he asked.

"It's not junk," Akima corrected him, with a hurt look in her eyes. "Come with me—I'll show you," she said and pulled him into the hallway.

"We had a deal," growled Korso as Cale and Akima approached his room. Curiously, they peeked in and on the transmitter was— the Drej queen!

Shocked, Cale and Akima turned to go, but Preed was blocking their way. Korso appeared in the doorway. "How long were they standing there?" he demanded.

"Long enough," Akima shot back.

"Akima! Come on!" Cale shouted and they took off through the ship, Preed and Korso right behind them. As they ran out into the drifter colony, Preed pulled out his gun and began to shoot. Akima was hit! Cale carried Akima to the safety of the drifter colony, and Korso and Preed took off in pursuit of the *Titan*.

Later, Akima awoke a little dazed. "How long was I out?"

"A few hours," Cale answered, looking back from the window.

Then she asked him about Korso, Preed, and the *Titan*. Cale looked determined, "Akima, we're gonna stop them."

Still hazy, Akima couldn't believe what she was hearing. "Cale, we don't even have a ship."

"Oh, we've got a ship," Cale replied, pointing out the window to the old ramshackle *Phoenix*.

"This thing's a wreck!" Akima declared, looking at it. It hadn't been flown in years.

Cale set to work fixing the ship and all of the colonists began to help. In no time, Cale and his new friends had the ship in working order. Cale and Akima hopped in the fixed-up *Phoenix*. All the colonists cheered as the ship lifted off, with Akima at the controls.

No sooner had they taken off when the *Valkyrie* radar was on to them.

"A ship. Three keks east. Human craft. Moving recklessly fast," Stith reported.

"Akima," Korso snarled. "Follow them!"

THE ICE RINGS

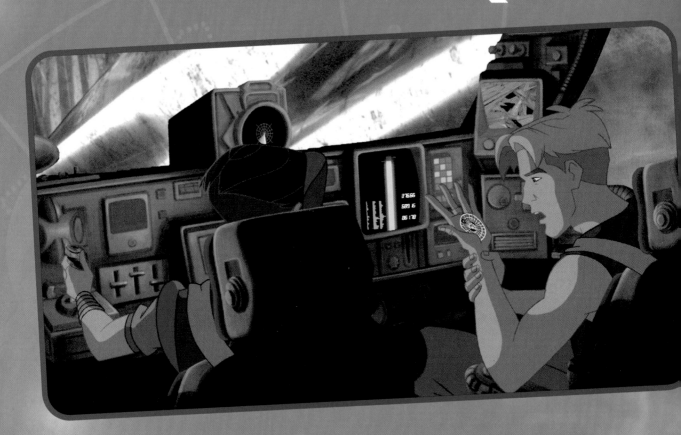

as Akima skillfully guided the *Phoenix* through the massive ice rings, Cale noticed that his hand had begun pulsing. "I think we're getting closer."

Just then, Akima caught a reflection of the *Valkyrie* mirrored in one of the ice crystals. "It's Korso!" she announced. "Right behind us."

The chase was on. The ships hurtled dangerously through space, narrowly missing spiraling chunks of ice. Finally, the *Valkyrie*—confused by reflections and trapped by ice—lost sight of the *Phoenix*.

With Korso off their tail, Akima and Cale powered on towards the *Titan*. Shooting through an icy tunnel, they emerged out into open space when Cale shouted, "Look there!"

OF TIGRIN

Akima swiftly turned the ship, and at long last, the enormous bronze orb of the *Titan* came into view.

"Have you ever seen *anything* like it?" Akima gasped.

"Just once," Cale remembered.

THE TITAN

as Cale and Akima entered the *Titan*, the hallway was lined with thousands of labeled vials. "DNA coding," Cale marveled. "These are animals, or they will be."

Cale approached the control platform and gasped. Cale saw his own toy invention from that day on the river. "Dad..." he whispered, thinking back

Cale looked down and saw an activation cone. Somehow, he knew this is where his ring belonged. The lights of the *Titan* turned on floor by floor and a hazy figure began to materialize above the control panel. It was Cale's father!

"If this message has been activated," Sam Tucker's image said, "then I have died before finding you. I wish I could be there." He continued, "This ship has the power to make a new planet, but the power cells are drained. It's up to you to restore their power."

Suddenly, a shot rang out cutting through Sam Tucker's voice.

"He always did talk too much," snapped Korso as he entered.

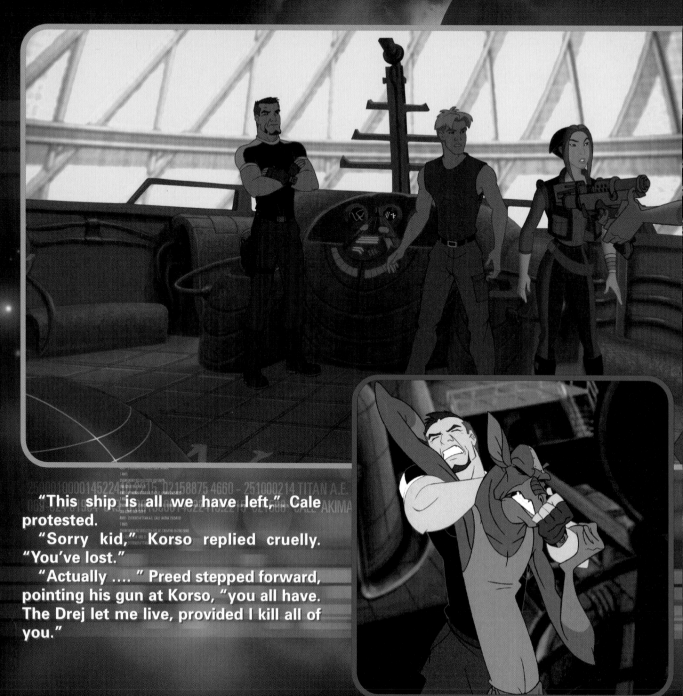

"This ship is all we have left," Cale protested.

"Sorry kid," Korso replied cruelly. "You've lost."

"Actually .... " Preed stepped forward, pointing his gun at Korso, "you all have. The Drej let me live, provided I kill all of you."

Suddenly, Korso dove towards the railing, distracting Preed. Akima jumped on Preed, but was thrown off. Then Cale lept on him and the two struggled. Finally, Korso attacked Preed from behind, dropping him to the floor.

Cale saw that Korso had snatched the ring from the control panel. "Give me the ring!" Cale shouted. They wrestled wildly, fighting for the ring. Falling over the railing, they landed on a catwalk. Without warning, it collapsed under them, and Korso dangled over the edge. Cale reached out his hand to save him, but Korso slipped, falling into the deep pit below.

Cale had just retrieved the ring from the ground when the *Titan* was rocked with enemy fire. They were under attack by the Drej. "Let's not panic," Cale said, trying to keep a cool head. Then an idea struck him. "The Drej are pure energy. And what do we need?" he asked.

"Energy!" Akima realized.

"I can re-route the system to use Drej energy," Cale explained and began fiddling with the control panel.

One of the circuits was broken. Cale had to risk going outside of the ship to work on it, and Akima had to cover him. Once outside Cale was under steady attack from Drej fire. Out of nowhere a lone figure appeared to save him, "Go ahead kid, I'll cover you." It was Korso!

The Drej stingers gathered in formation, "Now we finish it!" hissed the Drej queen.

Just then, Korso dove towards the damaged breaker and shoved in a metal bar—completing the circuit. The deadly Drej energy beam shot through him and the circuit.

"It's absorbing usssssssss…" cried the fading Mother Drej.

The transformation sequence was activated! As it spun wildly, gas and dust began to form—then land and water. The new planet was beginning.

"This is amazing," Akima whispered, staring out over the new planet.

"I know," Cale replied, staring out in wonder.

Just then the *Valkyrie* shot by overhead, with Stith and Gune waving wildly. Cale and Akima waved back and smiled. At long last, they had a new home.